בס"ד

This book belongs to:

לה' הארץ ומלואה

Please read it to me!

Hachai

THIRTY-ONE CAKES

A Hashavas Aveidah Story

by Loren Hodes

illustrated by Harvey Klineman

Hachai
PUBLISHING

Dedicated to Levana,
Aishes Chayil extraordinaire.
With blessings for good health and good spirit.
Her Family

***

Thirty-One Cakes
A Hashavas Aveidah Story

For Robin, my partner in rhyme, and our special children. L.H.

First Edition - Iyar 5763 / May 2003

Copyright © 2003 by **HACHAI PUBLISHING**
All Rights Reserved

Editor: D.L. Rosenfeld

ISBN: 1-929628-13-7
LCCN: 2002111978

HACHAI PUBLISHING
Brooklyn, New York
Tel 718-633-0100 Fax 718-633-0103
www.hachai.com   info@hachai.com

Printed in China

Glossary

Bubby - Grandmother
Hashavas Aveidah - Commandment to return lost items
Imma - Mother
Kosher - In accordance with Jewish dietary laws
Mitzvah - Commandment, good deed
Shul - Synagogue
Tzedakah - Charity

"Estie," called Imma,
"Get ready for fun,
It's time to bake cakes now;
We'll make thirty-one!

"At our shul we will sell
All the cakes that we bake,
And tzedakah will get
All the money we make."

Estie felt so excited;
She started to sing,
Baking all kinds of cakes
Was her favorite thing!

She took off her ring,
All shiny and gold,
That she got as a gift
When she turned six years old.

Estie scrubbed her hands well
With soap and warm water,
And Imma was pleased
With her very big daughter.
"I'm so glad," Estie said,
"That I'm big enough,
To help out with baking
And all kinds of stuff!"

She scooped out the sugar;

She sifted the flour;

She mixed and she measured
for over an hour.

Soon crunchy nut brownies and yellow sponge cake
And dark chocolate batter had started to bake.

Coffee cakes, marble cakes, swirly and sweet –

Piled up with banana cakes, ready to eat!

When Estie was finished, she looked all around,
But her precious gold ring just could not be found.

Tears filled Estie's eyes and rolled right down her face,
"Oh, how could my ring have been moved from its place?"

With Imma, she emptied
each pan and each pot;

They searched through the kitchen
in every last spot.

They checked on the windowsills, looked left and right,
But Estie's gold ring was nowhere in sight.

Then Estie turned pale, and she cried out, "Oh no!
I'm sure that my ring fell right into the dough!
It's baked in a cake; which one can it be?
Should we cut up all thirty-one cakes just to see?"

"Of course not," said Imma, "Let's think of a plan,
To get your ring back just as fast as we can."

"I know!" Estie smiled, feeling suddenly better,
"Why don't we sell every cake with a letter?"

So Estie wrote:

ב"ה

Enjoy this treat,
You've bought delicious cake to eat.
You also have a chance to do
A very special mitzvah, too.
While I was helping Imma bake,
My birthday ring fell in a cake.

Hashavas Aveidah, returning lost things
Surely goes for returning lost rings.
So if you feel your cake go crunch,
That's my ring you're about to munch.
Return it please; it's not too late,
And do a mitzvah that's truly great!

The tzedakah cake sale had never been better;
Estie sold all of her cakes with the letter.
"Now it's time," Estie said, "to wait and to see,
Who will be bringing my ring back to me?"

On that first afternoon, Estie waited and sat,
The phone didn't ring; she got tired of that.
The second day came; it was so hard to wait,
Then the third day went by; it grew dark and late.

But Estie was strong, and she didn't start moping,
No matter what, Estie wouldn't stop hoping.
"Someone with Hashavas Aveidah to do,
Is someone I'm certain will really come through!"

Then late in the evening of day number four
Estie heard somebody knock on the door.

Imma opened it up and said, "Well, hello!"
To four people standing there all in a row.

They came in the house to be welcomed and greeted;
One man began speaking when they were all seated.

"My name's Mister Katz,
  And it happened one day,
  That I hopped on a bus
  That was going my way.
  I looked down and saw
  A most wonderful cake
  That someone had left
  And forgotten to take.

"I wonder who lost it?" I heard myself say,
"I'll return it tomorrow and make someone's day."

"So I went to the bus station; there was a note—
A short simple message that somebody wrote:

"I rode on a bus to the end of the line,
   Which is where I met Rabbi and Mrs. Fine.
   I gave them the box and said, "Here is your cake.""

They answered, "It's not ours; there's been a mistake.
We found this on a plane in our overhead rack,
Now let's search for the owner, and give the cake back!"

"We went to the airport to look for a clue,
And saw a note telling us just what to do.
It said:

"The next day we drove out to Blueberry Lane,
  And that's where we met our new friend, Bubby Shain.
  We gave her the cake, and she said with a smile,
  'Thank you so much, won't you stay for a while?'"

"So we sat down together for tea and a snack,
To eat up the lost and found cake we brought back.
As we unwrapped the cake, we read Estie's letter,

Hashavas Aveidah – There's nothing that's better!
Then Bubby Shain had the surprise of her life,
When that ring came right out on the tip of her knife!"

"I'm so grateful," said Estie, "for all you have done."
She said 'thank you' again and again to each one.

With a smile just as shiny as her golden ring,
Estie said, "When I wear this, I'll think of one thing:
Someone with Hashavas Aveida to do,
Is someone I'm certain will really come through!"